The Broody Hen

OLIVIER DUNREA

The Broody Hen

A Doubleday Book for Young Readers

The illustrations are watercolor, executed on 140-pound hot press d'Arches watercolor paper.
Color borders are Canson Mi-Teintes paper. The typeface is 16-point Bernhard Modern. Typography by Cecilia Yung.
A DOUBLEDAY BOOK FOR YOUNG READERS
Published by Delacorte Press, Bantam Doubleday Dell Publishing Group, Inc., 666 Fifth Avenue, New York, New York 10103
Doubleday and the portrayal of an anchor with a dolphin are trademarks of Bantam Doubleday Dell Publishing Group, Inc.

Library of Congress Cataloging in Publication Data • Dunrea, Olivier. The broody hen / Olivier Dunrea.   p.   cm.
Summary: After several unsuccessful attempts, the broody hen lays a clutch of eggs and hatches them, and out pops speckled peepers.
I S B N 0 - 3 8 5 - 3 0 5 9 7 - 4   [I. Chickens—Fiction.]   I. Title.   PZ7.D922Br 1992 [E]—dc20   91-29377 CIP AC

Manufactured in the United States of America   October 1992   10 9 8 7 6 5 4 3 2 1

For
Dennis McGlade,
who broods

There once was a hen
a broody hen, a moody hen
who hatched a clutch of eggs.

That broody hen, that moody hen
marched to the windmill.
She flew to the rafters and laid an egg.
She laid an egg, a speckled brown egg.
That broody hen, that moody hen
laid a brown speckled egg.

But the egg rolled off and broke.

That broody hen, that moody hen
marched to the piggery.
She hopped into the feed trough and laid an egg.
She laid an egg, a speckled blue egg.
That broody hen, that moody hen
laid a blue speckled egg.

But the egg rolled off and broke.

That broody hen, that moody hen
marched to the dovecote.
She flew to the roof and laid an egg.
She laid an egg, a speckled rose egg.
That broody hen, that moody hen
laid a rose speckled egg.

But the egg rolled off and broke.

That broody hen, that moody hen
marched to the barn.
She hopped in the hayrack and laid an egg.
She laid an egg, a speckled gray egg.
That broody hen, that moody hen
laid a gray speckled egg.

But the egg rolled off and broke.

That broody hen, that moody hen
marched to the farmhouse.
She flew to a shelf and laid an egg.
She laid an egg, a speckled green egg.
That broody hen, that moody hen
laid a green speckled egg.

But the egg rolled off and broke.

That broody hen, that moody hen
marched to the farmer.
She hopped onto his hat and laid an egg.
She laid an egg, a speckled white egg.
That broody hen, that moody hen
laid a white speckled egg.

But the egg rolled off and broke.

The farmer took that broody hen, that moody hen
and marched her to the broody pen.
That broody hen, that moody hen slowly walked into the broody pen.
She scratched backward, she scratched forward.
She fluffed her feathers, she puffed her feathers, then she sat.
That broody hen, that moody hen sat in the broody pen and laid an egg.
She laid an egg, a speckled brown egg.

Beside the brown speckled egg she laid an egg.

She laid an egg, a speckled blue egg.

That broody hen, that moody hen laid a blue speckled egg.

Beside the brown speckled egg and the blue speckled egg
she laid an egg.

She laid an egg, a speckled rose egg.

That broody hen, that moody hen laid a rose speckled egg.

Beside the brown speckled egg, the blue speckled egg,

and the rose speckled egg she laid an egg.

She laid an egg, a speckled gray egg.

That broody hen, that moody hen laid a gray speckled egg.

Beside the brown speckled egg, the blue speckled egg,

the rose speckled egg, and the gray speckled egg she laid an egg.

She laid an egg, a speckled green egg.

That broody hen, that moody hen laid a green speckled egg.

Beside the brown speckled egg, the blue speckled egg,
the rose speckled egg, the gray speckled egg,
and the green speckled egg, she laid an egg.
She laid an egg, a speckled white egg.
That broody hen, that moody hen laid a white speckled egg.

Beside the brown speckled egg, the blue speckled egg,

the rose speckled egg, the gray speckled egg,

the green speckled egg, and the white speckled egg

she laid many more speckled eggs.

That broody hen, that moody hen laid many more speckled eggs.

Then that broody hen, that moody hen brooded and sat
on all those eggs, those speckled eggs.
That broody hen, that moody hen sat for twenty-one days.
Then she heard a cheep, she heard a peep.
That broody hen, that moody hen clucked to her eggs,
those speckled eggs, and the eggs cheeped and peeped back.

Out of those eggs popped speckled peepers!
That broody hen, that moody hen clucked and fussed,
fussed and clucked over all those peepers,
those speckled peepers.

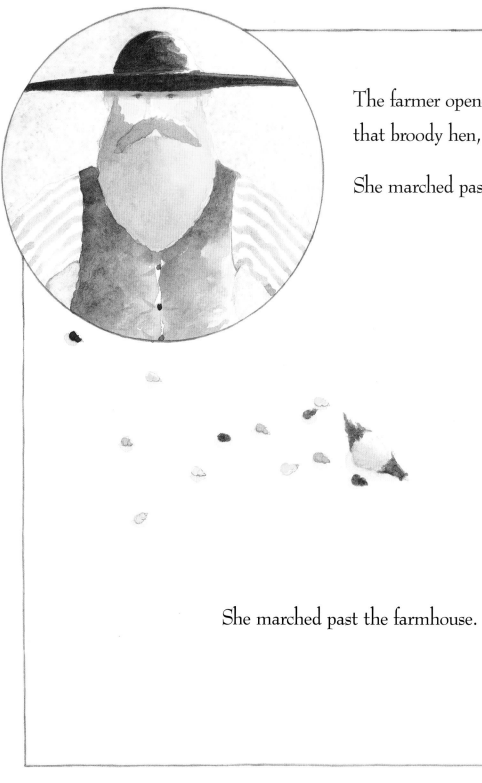

The farmer opened the broody pen and out marched that broody hen, that moody hen.

She marched past the farmer.

She marched past the farmhouse.

She marched past the barn.

She marched past the dovecote.

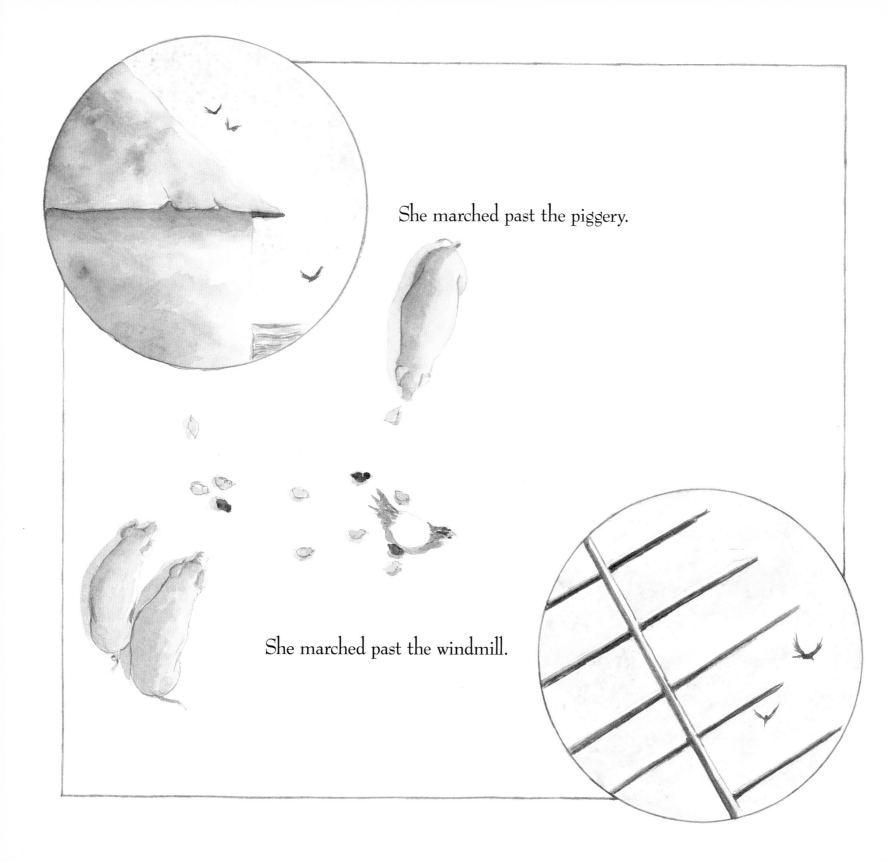

She marched past the piggery.

She marched past the windmill.

That broody hen, that moody hen
was followed by her brood.
They marched to the chicken yard and scratched and clucked,
clucked and scratched, scratched and peeped,
peeped and scratched.

There once was a hen
a broody hen, a moody hen
who hatched a clutch of eggs.